ISHI'S
‹ TALE OF LIZARD ›

Translated by Leanne Hinton

Illustrations by Susan L. Roth

Farrar · Straus · Giroux
New York

For my daughter, Jessy
—L.H.

To Duby with love,
and special thanks to Mr. and Mrs. Saburo Yuasa
and Mr. Takuji Sugimura
—S.L.R.
◀ ▶

Acknowledgments

There are so many people whose work helped lead the way to this book that actual authorship is difficult to assign. This is a set of excerpts from a tale that was told by Ishi in 1915 at the Berkeley, California, home of the anthropologist T. T. Waterman. He told it to Edward Sapir, renowned linguist and anthropologist, who wrote it down in Yahi and then worked with Ishi on a partial translation. Much later, Sapir's notebooks containing Ishi's tales were inherited by Alfred Kroeber, head anthropologist at the University of California at Berkeley. After Kroeber's death, his wife, Theodora Kroeber, organized his papers and deposited them at the Bancroft Library on the Berkeley campus. In a project initiated by linguist Victor Golla and funded by a grant from the National Science Foundation in 1986, Leanne Hinton coordinated a working group in the Department of Linguistics at Berkeley to undertake the task of analyzing and translating Ishi's tales. Ken Whistler developed computer programs for the project and did much of the preliminary grammatical analysis of the texts; research assistant Jean Perry entered them on the computer, performed further analysis, and did the first draft of the translations. Herb Luthin worked on details of later drafts of the translation of "Lizard," and Kay Luthin provided editorial suggestions. Leanne Hinton developed this children's version of "Lizard."

Translation copyright © 1992 by Leanne Hinton
Illustrations copyright © 1992 by Susan L. Roth
Library of Congress catalog card number: 92-6744
Published simultaneously in Canada by HarperCollins*CanadaLtd*
Color separations by Imago Publishing Ltd.
Printed in the United States of America
by Berryville Graphics
Designed by Martha Rago
First edition, 1992

◄ INTRODUCTION ►

Once there was a child named Ishi. He was a member of the Yahi tribe, a branch of the Yana people who lived in California in the nineteenth century and for thousands of years before that. They made their homes between the Mill Creek and Deer Creek drainages in the northeastern foothills bordering the Sacramento Valley. When the Gold Rush brought hordes of miners and settlers to California, Native American people suffered terribly, and most of Ishi's tribe were killed by white men. When Ishi was nine or ten years old, he and his few remaining relatives went into hiding. For more than forty years, they lived quietly and secretly in the wilderness around Deer Creek, staying in well-camouflaged brush huts, and keeping carefully out of sight of the few white people who came through their land. During that time, they made bows and arrows and fish spears out of the natural materials around them, hunted and fished with these tools, and made baskets to collect pine nuts and prepare acorn meal. They lived in the traditional way of their tribe, while the world outside their hiding place was changing.

Many years later, Ishi came alone out of the wilderness. It was August 1911. Ishi's last surviving relative, his mother, had died almost four years before, and he still wore his hair burned short in mourning. When he walked out of the forest into the town of Oroville that day, he probably believed he would be killed. Instead, the outside world was now ready to treat him with intense curiosity rather than hostility. He went to live in a museum in San Francisco, where he worked with anthropologists. That is how we know about his life.

One of the things he did was recite to the anthropologists stories that his family used to tell on winter nights. They were long, long stories, and the one you are about to read is only a set of selected parts of the whole tale that Ishi told. Ishi did not speak much English, even after he had lived in San Francisco for some time. He told his tales in his own language, Yahi, and anthropologists wrote down what he said, using a phonetic alphabet. The tale you are reading here is a translation, which we have tried to make as true as possible to the words that Ishi used.

This tale has no real beginning or end. It has little nuggets of stories in it; but what Ishi filled his telling with most of all was loving, detailed accounts of daily life as he had lived it. When you read the part about the hero, Lizard, making arrows or gathering pine nuts or dancing, you must remember that Ishi was talking about things that he had done himself over and over again, or that his relatives had done before they went into hiding. The "Yawi" who figure as enemies in the story are probably the Wintu, whom the Yana had sometimes fought. Ishi had also lived some of the more adventurous parts of the story himself, so when you read the part about Lizard killing the bear, remember this: Ishi in real life once killed a bear, too!

Even though this is a story from a completely different culture, there are pieces of it that might be familiar to you. Perhaps you have heard a version of "Little Red Riding-hood" that has some of the same events in it as the part of the tale that is about Lizard and Grizzly Bear. This story and others that Ishi knew were told for thousands of years without ever being written down. Some phrases are repeated a lot, and there is a rhythm in the telling that makes it something like a poem. Read it out loud if you have a chance to; it sounds best that way.

—Leanne Hinton
University of California
Berkeley

L izard.
He made arrows,
He worked at his arrowmaking.

At dawn, he smoothed down the arrow-shaft canes.
He made arrows.
He rubbed the arrow shafts smooth,
He worked at his arrowmaking,
    That's what he did.
He fitted the main shafts onto the foreshafts,
    That's what he did.
He socketed the foreshafts into the main shafts.
He spun the arrows on the ground.
He painted bands on them.
Now he worked at this, all day.
He feathered the arrows,
    That's what he did.
And then he trimmed the feathers,
    That's what he did.
He charred the feathers black.
He bound the arrows tight,
    That's what he did.
Now he scoured the shafts smooth.
He finished and put them aside at night.

At dawn,
"I have no more foreshaft wood," he said.
"Let Long-Tailed Lizard get it," he said.
"You go ahead to get foreshaft wood," he said.
And then Long-Tailed Lizard went to get foreshaft wood,
He now went off.
He twisted the foreshaft sticks out of the ground,
Now he broke them off.
He put them down on the ground with ashes.
"There are only a few sticks," he said.

Grizzly Bear jumped up!
She took and ate him!
She swallowed him down.
She turned,
And headed along the trail.

When it was just nightfall, Lizard went after the foreshaft wood,
Taking his quiver.
There was the foreshaft wood,
It lay on the ground.
He looked all over.
Sure enough, there were Grizzly Bear's tracks.
"Long-Tailed Lizard, did you get eaten?" he said.
He picked up the foreshaft sticks,
Carried them in his arms, and arrived home.

In the morning,
"What shall I do?" Lizard cried.
And then, grieving, he cut off his hair.
He took pitch,
And painted his face with it in mourning.
"Bear, now how long will it take for you to come?" he said.
"Aren't you hungry now?" he said.
He put a wild grapevine around his neck as a necklace.
He smoked,
Putting tobacco into his pipe.
"How long before you come here?" he said.
"Back to this eating place of yours?" he said.
He climbed up the grapevine tree,
Seated himself up in the grapevine tree.
Nightfall,
Dawn.
He waited.

"Let us go back west," said Bear.
  Now the grizzly bears went back west.
  The female was filled with Long-Tailed Lizard.
  Lizard heard them in the east.
"It must be them," he said.
"Now they have come from the east to get wild grapes to eat."
  The grapevine was hanging down from the top of the tree,
      his necklace.
  The bears pulled down on the vine.
"Are you pulling at me, you who have taken away my relative?
  It will be good if you die!" Lizard said.
"Put me on your back," he said.
  He unstrung his bowstring.
"Let it be you who comes to pack me on your back," he said.
  The one who had Long-Tailed Lizard inside went up to him.
  He tied his bowstring in the form of a lasso.
  He doubled the string into a circle.
  He pressed himself onto her back from above.
  Grizzly Bear came down again.
  She fell down to the ground strangled.

He took Long-Tailed Lizard, still alive, out of the dead Grizzly Bear.
He placed him in the water.
He bathed him.
He picked up his quiver,
Put Long-Tailed Lizard into the quiver.
He arrived home.
He threw away what had been his necklace,
And arrived home.

At dawn,
He took his arrow shafts
And laid them out.
He rubbed them smooth.
"What's the matter?" he said.
The arrow broke,
It broke in two.
Now he just sat there, expecting something to happen.
People came and told him, "The Dwarf People are dancing.
A dance is being held," he was told.
"Ah,
And you are telling me about it," he said.
"The arrow being smoothed just broke while I was working with it.
So they are dancing there!" he said.
He put away his arrowmaking things.

At sundown,
"Make a fire!" Lizard said.
"I'll do the Play-Dance!" he said.
Now he danced.
The Dwarf Women danced.
The Dwarf Women stopped dancing.
Now he sang,
Sang the lead.
They sang the rhythm part.
Now he sang along,
And they danced.
Then,
"Stop dancing, children!" he said.
Then again,
"Play-dance!" he said.
"Sing," he said,
"Your Play-Dance song!"
The dancers sang.
Then,
"Woman-dance!" he said.
"Hene ya, Pane ya,
Hh, hh, hi ya,
Say that!" he said.
"Sing the rhythm, children!
Say your song!" he said.
Now they danced and danced.
"Say it, children!" he said.

Dancing, they flowed to the south,
They flowed to the north.
"Ch, ch, hi ya," he said.
"Sing in accompaniment!
Say it, children!" he said.
"Play-dance!" he said.

Later,
"Now stop dancing," he said.
"Sleep, all of you children."

At dawn, he arose.

"It is not good to sleep late," said Lizard.

The women went back to the house.

They washed themselves.

He took up his arrowmaking things.

He rubbed the arrows smooth.

He socketed the foreshafts into the main shafts, all day,
    That's what he did.

Now he painted on bands, all day.

He put them down, finished.

Now he feathered the arrows,

Now worked at the feathering of arrows,
    That's what he did.

He turned the arrows on the ground.

He trimmed off the vanes with obsidian,
    That's what he did.

He charred the feathers black,
    That's what he did.

He put them away.

He slung over his shoulder the deer horns

Made into a quiver.

He had cut them off at the stump,

The deer horns.

He put the arrows into the quiver.

"Go off to gather food, children!"

And then his flints.
He chipped out flakes.
Now he kept flaking off chips,
All day.
He put food into a basket.
"Eat, children!" he said, at night.
Now they ate their meal.
They finished eating.

At dawn,
Lizard took his quiver and his storage baskets.
Now he went west,
Went west across the water,
Went west up the mountain.
He put his quiver down on the ground.
He climbed up to get pine nuts.
He climbed back down.
And then he piled pine-nut cones all around the fire.
Now he worked at pounding,
He pounded the pinecones for nuts,
    That's what he did.
He picked up his storage basket,
Picked up still another basket,
And now he gathered up the nuts.
He took them up in his hands.

A great sound descended.
The Yawi shouted their war whoops.
"Ho, I think
It is the wind," he said,
Pretending to ignore them.
"It looks like rain now.
I'd better sit here and shell nuts," he said.
He picked up his storage basket.
"I see you on the ground everywhere!" he said to the nuts.
He slung his basket over his shoulder
And carried it under his arm.
He took his bow.
Now he went along the trail.

He shot off arrows.
He shot to the east,
He shot to the south,
He shot to the north.
Now he went on along the trail.
He shot off arrows.
He hit straight into their faces.
He went back home, going into the water,
He came back out of the water.
The Yawi scattered out of sight.
Now he went on along the trail, at sundown.
He went on along the trail.
"Here are lots of pine nuts," he said.
"Seems like rain out there, in the wind," he said.

There is no more.
Now the talking stops.

DATE DUE			